If Only I Had A Pet Elephant

WRITTEN BY
J.P. ANTHONY WILLIAMS

DREAM WEAVER TALES

Thank You - Your <u>Free</u> Gift

Thank you for your interest in "If Only I Had A Pet Elephant". You can download your exclusive <u>FREE</u> copy of this amazing <u>Animals Coloring Book</u> by scanning the QR code with your phone camera

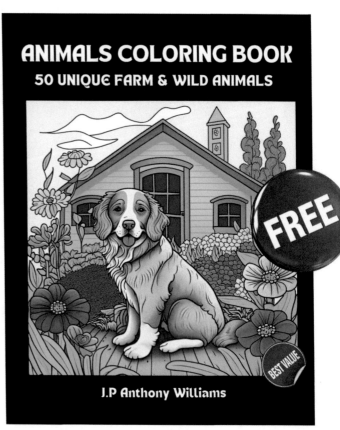

Scan QR Code for other Books in this Series

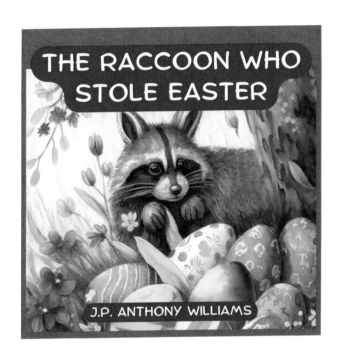

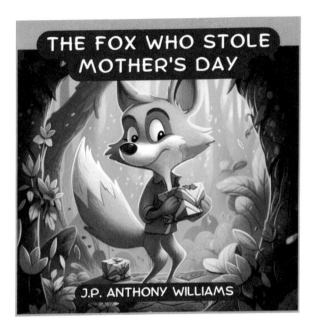

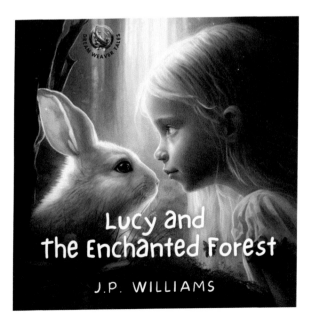

DAY AT THE CIRCUS

CIRCUS

It's a beautiful summer day, and Liam and Emma are super excited.
They are going to the circus today with their mother.

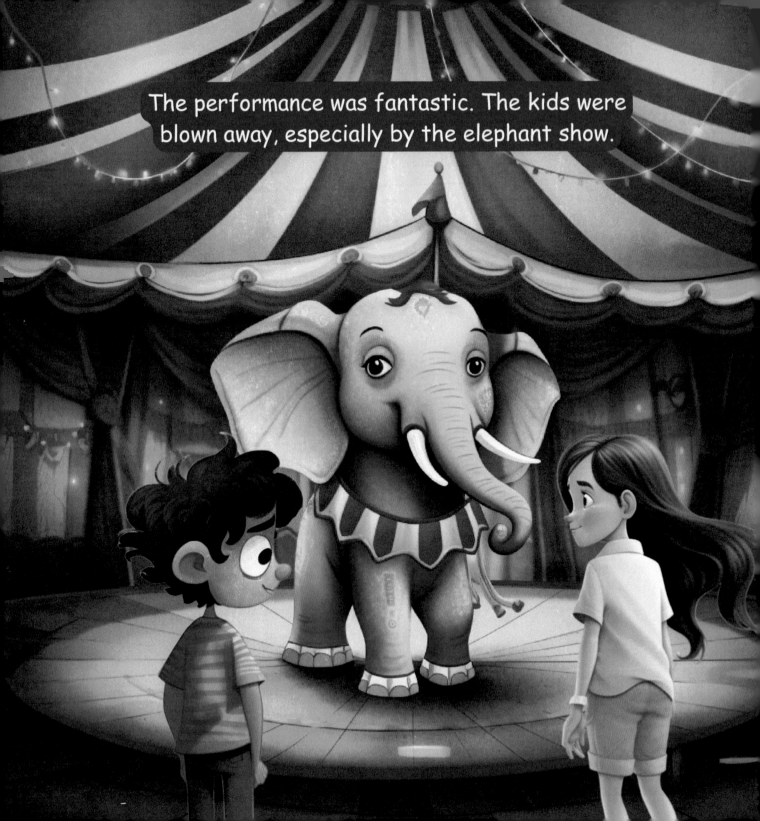

The performance was fantastic. The kids were blown away, especially by the elephant show.

Liam and Emma jumped up with big smiles on their faces, as Felix led the way.

In search of a pet, the kids dreamed big,
An elephant to ride, oh, what a gig!
But soon they learned, with grateful eyes,
Their furry cat, Felix, was the ultimate prize.

THE END

Check out the next book in this series

Thank You - Your _Free_ Gift

Thank you for reading **"If Only I Had a Pet Elephant"**.

I hope you enjoyed it and if you have a minute to spare, I would be extremely grateful if you could post <u>a short review on my book's Amazon page</u>

To show my gratitude, I am offering a **FREE** copy of this amazing <u>Animals Coloring Book.</u> Download your free copy by scanning the QR code or clicking the link

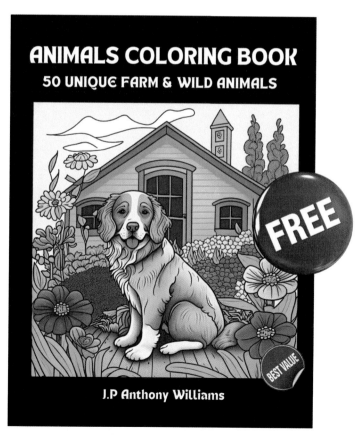

What's Next ?

Scan QR Code for other Books in this Series

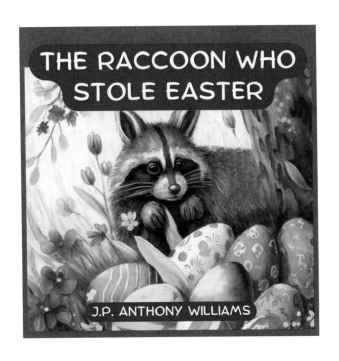

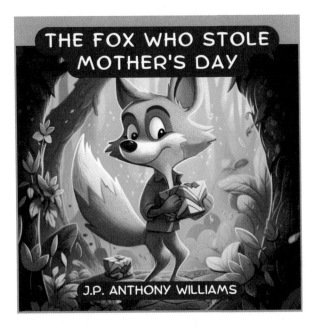

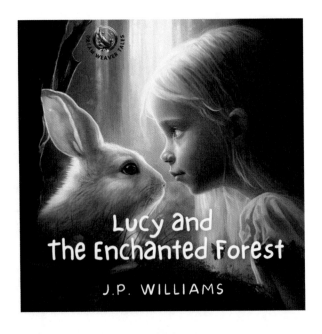

What's Next ?

Scan QR Code for other Books in this Series

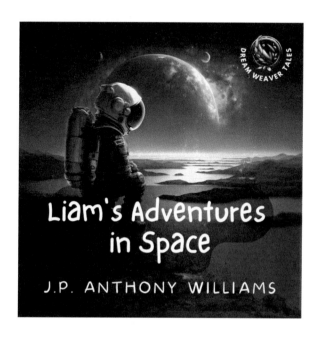

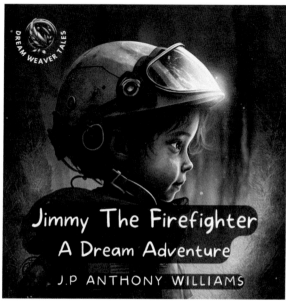

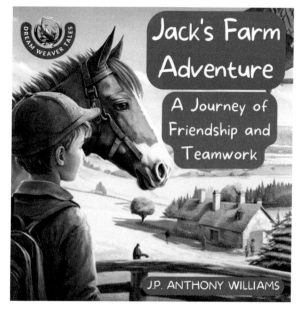

About the Author

J.P Anthony Williams is a bestselling children's book author, known for his enchanting tales and vivid illustrations. His stories are loved by young readers all over the world.

Born and raised in a small town, J.P developed a love of nature and storytelling at an early age. He spent his childhood exploring the woods and fields near his home, and he loved nothing more than curling up with a good book.

J.P's stories are known for their vivid imagery and richly-detailed illustrations. He takes inspiration from the natural world and from the myths and legends of his childhood, and he weaves them into tales that are both entertaining and educational.

In his free time, J.P can be found exploring new places and seeking inspiration for his next book. He is also a big advocate for environmental conservation, and often uses his platform to raise awareness about nature and its preservation.

Special thanks to my wife and kids for their endless support.

Made in the USA
Middletown, DE
05 September 2023